Violet and Victor write
the Best-Ever
Bookworm
Book

Written by Alice Kuipers

Illustrated by Bethanie Deeney Murguia

LITTLE, BROWN AND COMPANY
NEW YORK   BOSTON

I'm Violet Small and I'm six minutes older than my twin brother.

I love writing and I'm a great speller.

I want to write the best-ever book in the whole entire world.

My name is Victor Small, but I am BIG.

Violet is my twin sister and she is very bossy.

She wants my help to write her book. She says I have good ideas.

I want to count my pet worms instead.

Enough about you
(and I am NOT bossy)!
Now, the story needs a beginning.

How about:

Wilbur is the biggest, strongest, bravest worm in the worm farm.

Wilbur should be called Violet.
And she's not a worm.

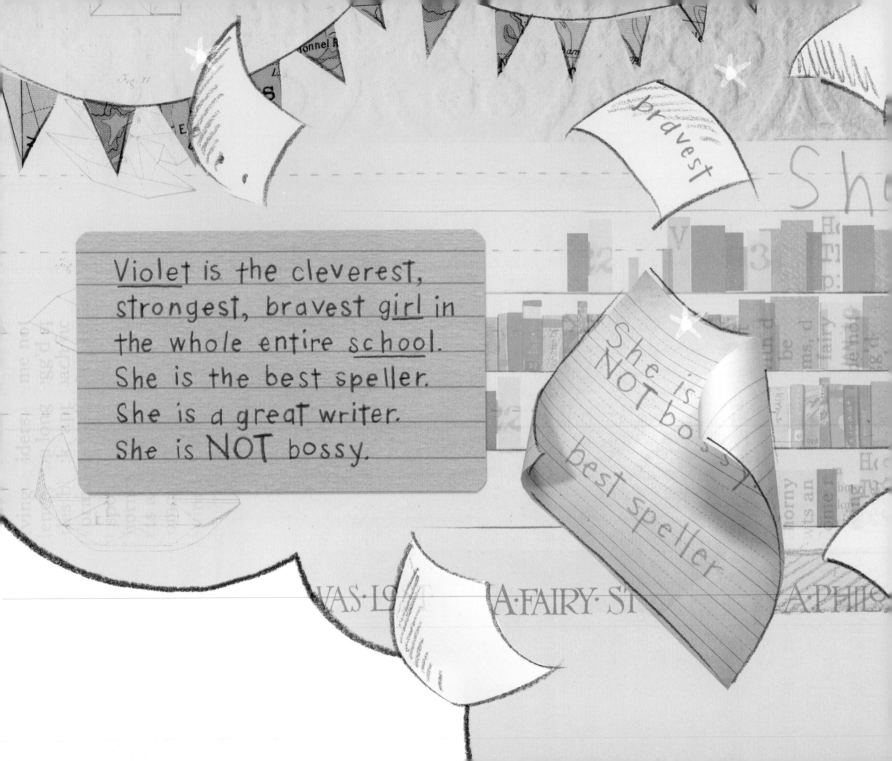

Violet is the cleverest, strongest, bravest girl in the whole entire school. She is the best speller. She is a great writer. She is NOT bossy.

I don't want to have
ideas anymore.
I want to—

One more line,
then you can hang out with
your dirty, squirmy worms.

Worms aren't dirty.
They *eat* dirt—

Not now, Victor.
One more line, PLEEEASE.

One day, Violet overhears the school librarian say, "This book is missing some pages."

Why?
Where are the pages?

Wait.
That's what the story's about.

I want to know NOW.

I'll spoil it, then:

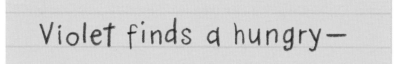
Violet finds a hungry—

NO!

Don't spoil it.

All right.

Violet hunts for
the book-eating
monster....

She creeps by
comic books.

WELCOME

She slips
through stories!

vine

She eyeballs encyclopedias.

Vegetables

Pole-beans
Tomatoes
Winter Squash (long), Summer Squash
  (short)
Pumpkins
Cucumbers

Vines

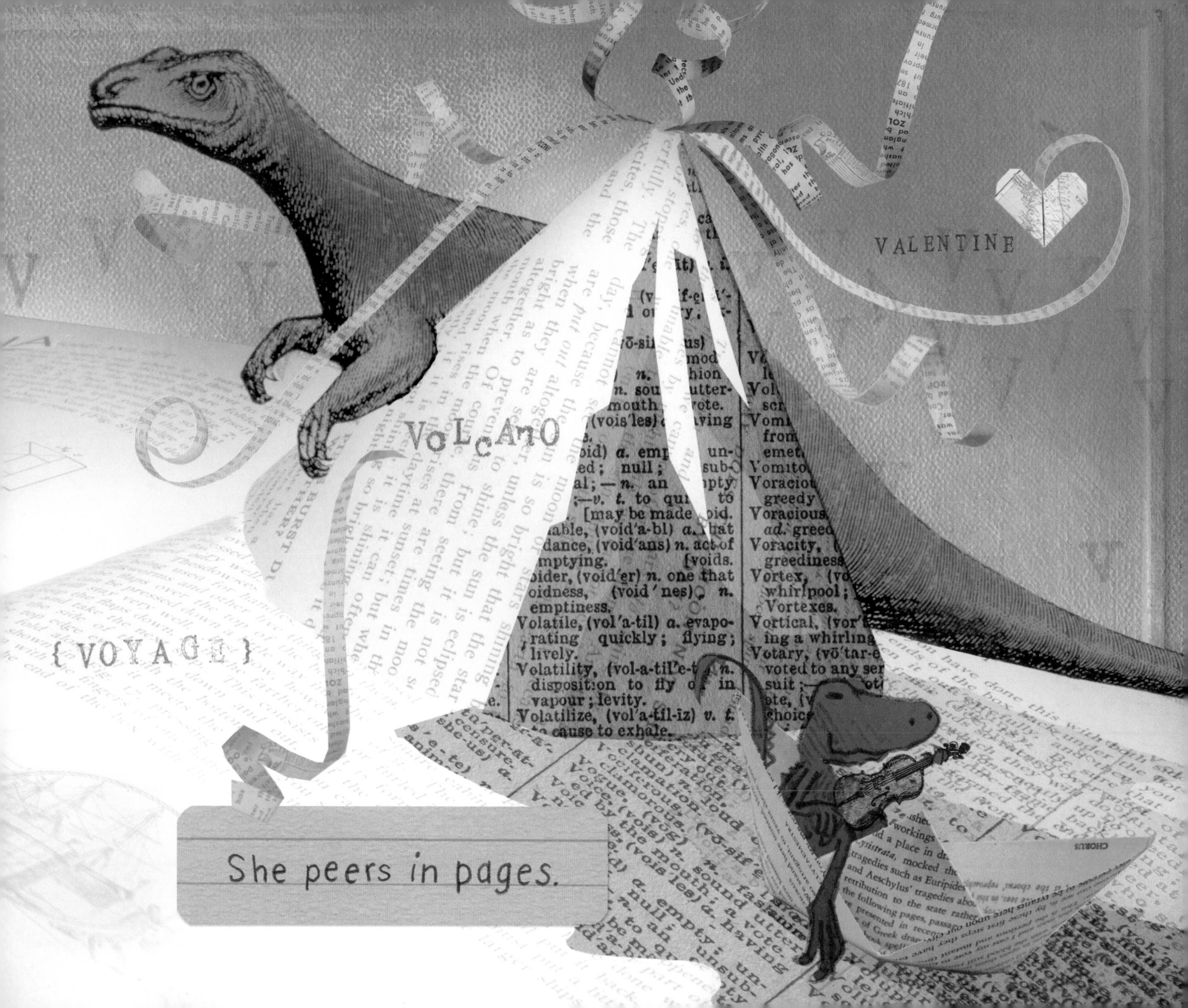
VALENTINE
VOLCANO
{ VOYAGE }

She peers in pages.

She flies through fairy tales,

but she can't find the terrible book-eating monster anywhere.

Where *is* it, Victor?

She hears a
snuffling by
her feet.

Stop, stop, stop! This isn't supposed to be SCARY. Scary books are horrible.

Don't worry. It's not scary.

There's a snuffle, a sniffle, and a squeak. From between her feet comes sneaking the smallest, hungriest...

Oooooh, Victor,
I LOVE this story.

I LOVE the bookworm.
It's so cute.
It's purple, with blue stripes,
big eyes, and fuzzy ears.

It's NOT purple. It's orange.
It's NOT fuzzy. It's spiky.
With no ears. Worms
don't have ears.

FIG. I.

Worms, 193
    bookworms, 193
defined, 209
mic position, 193
orms, 193
worms, 193
worms, 193
rms, 193
193

Fig. 1
Bookworm, (book'wurm) n.

NO, it's my bookworm
because it's MY book.

The bookworm is busy munching books. Violet has to save the library. So she tucks the bookworm into her pocket and takes it home.

592.64

49

Where she asks her brother for good ideas.

Then Violet writes brilliant books for the bookworm.

The bookworm gobbles up—

NO! The bookworm shouldn't eat books anymore.

Violet reads her books out loud. The bookworm fills up on the words it hears.

It should eat raw dirt.

I like my idea better.

The bookworm is
stuffed full of stories.

BOOKS BY VIOLET

Violet is the best writer in the whole entire world. And she is the best reader. And she is the best speller (and she is NOT bossy). The library is saved. The bookworm is never hungry again.

I like our book.

Our book?

Will you read it to me?
Like I'm a hungry bookworm.

I'm a bookworm too.
We're both fuzzy, hungry bookworms.

I'm not fuzzy. I'm SPIKY and—

Shh. Let's read.

For Theo, Lola, and Felix
—A. K.

For my brothers
—B. D. M.

•Library of Congress Cataloging-in-Publication Data•Kuipers, Alice, 1979–
•Violet and Victor write the best-ever bookworm book / by Alice Kuipers;
illustrated by Bethanie Deeney Murguia. — First edition.•pages cm•Summary:
When Violet decides to write a book, she insists that her twin brother help
because he has good ideas, but Victor would rather count his pet worms.
•ISBN 978-0-316-21200-7•[1. Authorship—Fiction. 2. Brothers and
sisters—Fiction. 3. Twins—Fiction.] I. Murguia, Bethanie
Deeney, illustrator. II. Title.•PZ7.K9490146Vi 2014
•[E]—dc23•2012048437•10 9 8 7 6 5 4 3 2 1•SC
•Printed in China